This book
belongs to:

Makayla

MESSAGE TO PARENTS

This book is perfect for parents and children to read aloud together. First read the story to your child. When you read it again, run your finger under each line, stopping at each picture for your child to "read." Help your child to figure out the picture. If your child makes a mistake, be encouraging as you say the right word. Point out the written word beneath each picture in the margin on the page. Soon your child will be "reading" aloud with you, and at the same time learning the symbols that stand for words.

Library of Congress Cataloging-in-Publication Data

Meltzer, Lisa.
The elephant's child / retold by Lisa Meltzer ; illustrated by Pat Stewart.
p. cm. — (A Read along with me book)
Summary: A rebus version of the Rudyard Kipling story that tells how elephants got their long trunks.
ISBN 0-02-898238-X :
[1. Elephants—Fiction. 2. Rebuses.] I. Stewart, Pat Ronson, ill. II. Kipling, Rudyard, 1865–1936. The elephant's child. III. Title. IV. Series.
PZ7.M51648E1 1989
[E]—dc19

89-631
CIP
AC

READ ALONG WITH ME books are conceived by Deborah Shine.
READ ALONG WITH ME is a registered trademark of Checkerboard Press, Inc.
Printed in the United States of America 0 9 8 7 6 5 4 3 (G1/10)

The Elephant's Child

A Read Along With Me Book

Retold by **Lisa Meltzer**
Illustrated by **Pat Stewart**

CHECKERBOARD PRESS
NEW YORK

elephants

one

elephant

Long ago in Africa, did not have trunks. They had only big bulgy noses that could wriggle. At that time there was 1 little child who asked ever so many questions.

He asked the  why her feathers grew just so. He asked the  why he had spots. So the ostrich and the giraffe spanked him. He asked the hippo why her eyes were red, and the hippo spanked him.

But still the  child asked questions! He asked about everything he saw, or heard, or felt, or smelled. And everyone spanked the  child.

ostrich

giraffe

hippo

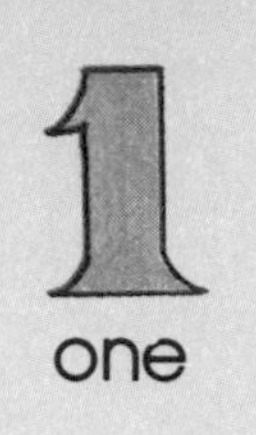

one

elephant

crocodile

animals

1 day the elephant child asked, "What does the crocodile eat for dinner?"

"HUSH!" said all the animals. And they spanked him for a very long time.

Now, the elephant child had never seen or heard or felt or smelled or

touched a  . All he knew was

that the   lived by the  .

"I will go to the river to ask what

the crocodile eats for dinner," he said.

"Good-bye," said all the  ,

and they spanked the  child

one more time for good luck.

The elephant child traveled for 

days. At last he came to the

jungle. There he met a  . It

was coiled around a  .

river

three

snake

tree

crocodile

elephant

snake

"Can you please tell me what the eats for dinner?" asked the child.

"What?" said the . And the spanked the little child.

The child did not like being spanked. So he said good-bye to the and he walked to the . There he stepped on a log of wood. But it was really the 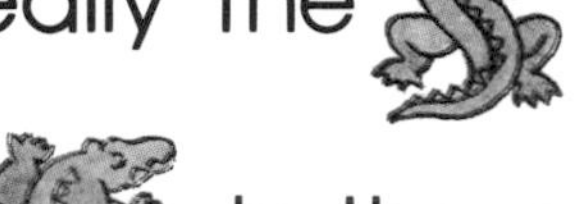 !

"Have you seen a in these parts?" asked the  child.

The lifted his tail out of the  . The child stepped back. He did not want to be spanked.

river

elephant

crocodile

"Come here, little  child," said the  . "I am the  ."

"Why, you are the very animal I am looking for," said the  child.

"Can you please tell me what you eat for dinner?"

"Come closer," said the  . "I will whisper the answer to you."

So the child put his head close to the musky, tusky mouth of the  .

"I think," said the , "today I will begin with child!" And he caught the child by his nose and pulled. The child was very surprised. Poor child! His nose began to stretch and stretch. This hurt more than a spanking!

snake

tree

elephant

one

The   scuffled down from the  . He knotted himself around the elephant child. "Pull, little  child!" said the  . The  child and the  pulled  way and

the  pulled the other way.

Poor  child! His nose stretched and stretched into a  . With a loud POP the  let go.

The child fell back. "Thank you," he said to the  . Then he hung his poor stretched  in the river to cool and shrink.

After 3 days, the 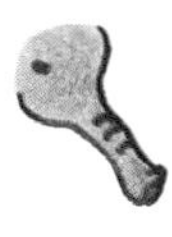 was cool. But it was still long. It was a real trunk just like  have today.

crocodile

trunk

elephant

river

three

elephants

fly

elephant

river

trunk

snake

By and by a landed on the child and stung him. The child lifted his trunk out of the and hit the .

"You could not have done that with your old ," said the .

"You are right," said the child. Then he started for home.

Across Africa he went, frisking and whisking his . He learned to do all kinds of things with it. He cooled his head with a schloop of mud. He sang a little song.

At last the child arrived home. The were glad to see him. "How do you do?" said the child.

animals

animals

elephant

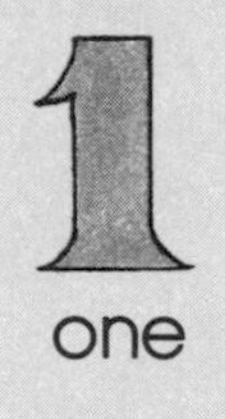

one

elephants

"Come here and be spanked for asking," the said.

"Pooh," said the child. "You know nothing about spanking, but I do." Then he knocked over of his brother .

"Oh, bananas!" they said. "What

have you done to your nose?"

"I got a new  from the 

who lives in the ," said the

child. "I asked him what he

eats for dinner, and he gave me this."

trunk

crocodile

river

animals

elephant

monkey

elephants

river

crocodile

"It is very ugly," said the  .

"But it is very useful," said the  child, and he picked up the  and threw him into a beehive.

Then that bad child spanked all the  for a long  time. Finally all the  hurried  off to the  to get new noses from the  . When they came back, nobody spanked anybody anymore. And ever since that day, all the [elephants] you will ever see,

and all those that you will not,

have trunks just like the trunk of

the little [elephant] child.

Words I can read

- ☐ animals
- ☐ crocodile
- ☐ elephant
- ☐ elephants
- ☐ fly
- ☐ giraffe
- ☐ hippo
- ☐ monkey
- ☐ one
- ☐ ostrich
- ☐ river
- ☐ snake
- ☐ three
- ☐ tree
- ☐ trunk